Farewell to Ireland

For Mona

First published in 1998 by Franklin Watts

This paperback edition published in 1999

Franklin Watts
96 Leonard Street
London EC2A 4XD

Franklin Watts Australia
14 Mars Road
Lane Cove
NSW 2066

Editor: Kyla Barber
Designer: Kirstie Billingham
Consultant: Margaret Ward, Research Fellow in History, Bath Spa University

A CIP catalogue record for this book is available from the British Library.

ISBN 0 7496 3448 0 (pbk)
0 7496 3094 9 (hbk)

Dewey Classification 941.5

Printed in Great Britain

Farewell to Ireland

by
Malachy Doyle
Illustrations by Greg Gormley

W
FRANKLIN WATTS
NEW YORK • LONDON • SYDNEY

1

An American Wake

The cottage was packed. Men, women and children lined the walls, on benches, stools and one another's knees. A fiddler was playing his heart out in the corner, and couples were raising the dust with their dancing.

It was an American wake. Young Mary Ellen and her little brother Frankie were going to New York in the morning, and all their friends and neighbours had gathered to see them off.

Mary Ellen left the crowded room and stepped outside under the stars, only to find her father there before her.

"Thanks for putting on such a good spread, Dad," she said quietly.

"Ah," said Michael Connolly, unable to hide the sadness in his voice, "sure you've been a good daughter to us,

Mary Ellen. It's the least we could do."

"I'll look after Frankie on the journey, Dad, and Jim's promised he'll be there to meet us. We'll be all right, you know."

Jim was their older brother, who'd left three years before. He'd done well for himself, and a month ago he'd sent the fares.

"Aye, that's as maybe," said Michael. "But you're awfully young to be leaving home. If I thought there was any sort of a decent life for you here in Ireland I'd never let you go."

"We'll be fine, Dad," said Mary Ellen. "And we'll still be with family."

There was a deep ache in her own heart too, but she was determined not to show it, not tonight at least. She'd made up her mind to leave, and that was that. There'd be plenty of time for crying later.

She went back into the other room, where people were gathered round a large table drinking tea, whiskey and stout and eating scones and soda bread.

Frankie was in the corner with some of his friends, boasting of the rare old times he'd be having in the big city of New York. The boys were hanging on to every word.

Sarah, Mary Ellen's mother, was serving the food, helped by the twins - the two younger girls who'd be staying at home with baby Liam.

"Sit down, Mother," said Mary Ellen. "Take the weight off your feet and I'll look after the guests."

"Ah no," said Sarah, "I couldn't be doing that. You're the one that's got the long journey ahead of you."

Soon someone shouted, "Daybreak!" The music stopped and the whole house went quiet.

"It is, too," said Michael, leading everyone outside. They stood in silence, watching the sun rise on Mary Ellen and Frankie Connolly's last day in Ireland.

2

Last Goodbyes

At ten in the morning, after a big breakfast of bacon and eggs that Sarah made them eat, it was time to leave. The guests had gone home hours ago, but they'd been drifting back to see the emigrants off. Frankie had on a new suit for the journey. Michael put his own cap on his son's head and went to fetch the cart.

Sarah took off her best shawl and wrapped it round her daughter.

"Look after yourself, love," she said, hugging her close. "And watch over the wee fellow for me. Keep an eye on his wandering, especially on the boat, for you know what he's like. And make sure he washes behind his ears!"

"Is it Frankie you mean?" said Mary Ellen, laughing. "Sure he's a great big strap of a lad, dressed in his Sunday best. But I'll keep him by me, day and night, don't you worry, Mammy. And he'll wash his neck every morning, on the boat and after, or I'll give him what for!"

"My wee girl and boy!" Sarah wailed. "What's to become of you, away over the ocean in a coffin ship like the one your Uncle Willy died on?"

The cottage filled with the sound of wailing, as one by one the other women joined in. Liam and the twins took up the cry –

even Frankie's dog by the hearth started to howl.

"How many times do I have to tell you, Mammy?" said Mary Ellen. "They have great big steamships now. The food's good, there's no fever and they don't sink. Sure, Jim got over, no trouble, and in two weeks we'll be there with him."

"God willing," said Sarah quietly. "But will you ever be back? Will I see you again in this life?"

She held both her children tight, searching their faces as if to fix them in her memory.

"God bless you both," she whispered, "and keep you safe."

The clatter of the cart was heard from outside.

"It's time," said Michael, coming into the room.

Frankie and Mary Ellen tore themselves from their mother's grip and left the house, wiping away their tears.

"You be good girls when I'm gone," said Mary Ellen, hugging the twins and kissing the baby. "Help Mammy round the house and work hard at school."

"And look after the dog for me," added Frankie.

The last thing Mary Ellen did before climbing up on to the cart was to pick up a sod of turf from the stack by the side of the house and slip it into her bag.

People ran down the road calling and waving and pressing food on to them for the journey. Oatcakes, salt beef and apples came from all sides.

"Thank you, thank you," said Mary Ellen, reaching out. "But you don't have to, you know. They do feed you on the boat these days . . ."

She bit her lip. She knew that even though the Famine was more than fifty years ago now, it always came back to people's minds at times like this. It was hard enough saying goodbye, without having to think of those terrible years when the potato crop failed four times out of five – when hunger cost the lives of over a million Irish people, and millions more fled the country, only for many to die of fever or shipwreck on the way.

Father drove the cart slowly until they reached the crossroads, so all the young ones could keep up as was the custom.

Then he stopped and there was another round of goodbyes, but this time it was less desperate. Sure, most of them would be following in Frankie and Mary Ellen's footsteps as soon as they could raise the money. Who'd stay in Ireland, when there were money and jobs galore over the water?

3

All Aboard!

Father took them by cart to the station and joined them on the long train journey across the country. He booked them all into a lodging house in Queenstown for their last night in Ireland, but precious little sleep came to either Frankie or Mary

Ellen, what with all the excitement and sadness.

The next morning they were standing on board the *Orlandia*, waving farewell to Ireland.

They'd watched from the docks with their hearts racing as the twin red funnels of the great Cunard liner appeared over the horizon, steaming its way into the harbour. Eventually, the Irish emigrants had boarded, watched by the passengers who'd got on at Liverpool and were already up on deck, waiting to set sail for America.

"They say Cunard hasn't lost a single life, nor even a letter, in over fifty years," Jim had written, to reassure their mother. "Frankie and Mary Ellen couldn't be in safer hands."

Nevertheless it was a heartsore Michael Connolly who watched his son and daughter sail into the distance, maybe for ever. Praying for a safe crossing, he wiped the tears from his eyes and turned for home.

Mary Ellen and Frankie didn't leave the deck until they'd passed the bar of the harbour and were out into the choppy waters of the open sea. Only when Ireland had gone from view, and all there was to be seen was the vast ocean, did either speak.

"Goodbye, my lovely island," whispered Mary Ellen before turning to her brother. "Come on, Frankie, grab your bags. We'd better find out where to go."

The boat was jam-packed. There were ladies and gentlemen dressed in fine cloaks and top hats parading around the deck as though they owned the place. There were poor folk shivering in nothing but rags, and people from distant lands in the oddest of clothes. It felt to Mary Ellen as though the whole world was on that boat.

She went up to a smart-looking couple, with a young boy about Frankie's age. "Excuse me, sir, ma'am. Would you know where we're supposed to sleep?" she asked.

"We are in the First Class section," said the man sharply, pointing towards the front of the ship. "I've no idea where your sort go."

"What's First Class?" asked Frankie when they'd gone.

"Oh, that'll be a special part of the boat for all the rich people," answered his sister. "Never you mind about them."

She asked a young woman carrying a baby, but she just looked at Mary Ellen helplessly, not understanding.

Eventually she saw a member of the ship's crew. "Where do we put our bags, sir?" she asked.

"Steerage, is it?" he said. Mary Ellen nodded.

"Follow me." He led them down two sets of stairs.

The dark airless room was lined with bunks, all pushed up next to one another. There were people everywhere, sitting on beds, floor, trunks, suitcases and blankets.

"You'll have to see if you can find any beds that haven't been taken," said the sailor, turning to leave.

Mary Ellen led Frankie up and down the lines of bunks. Those that didn't have someone on them were covered in baskets, sacks or battered suitcases. At last they found two, one above the other, at the far end of the long room. They put their bags on the floor and lay down.

"I bet it's not like this in First Class," muttered Frankie.

It took Mary Ellen a long time to get to sleep, what with the coughing of old men, the crying of babies, the smell of fish, tobacco, sweat and seasickness, but she was exhausted from the journey and at last she fell asleep.

4

Making Friends

Mary Ellen woke in the early evening to the hustle and bustle of mealtime. Everyone was rushing to the tables in the middle of the room, and sailors were bringing in food. People were talking in many languages: Irish, English and Welsh,

she guessed, never mind what else.

She went to wake Frankie, but he wasn't in his bunk. He came down the steps just as she sat down at a table next to a family who were chattering away to one another in a strange language.

"Where have you been, Frankie?" she asked. "I was worried about you."

"Oh, just having a look round," he answered.

"Well you're not to go off without telling me again. Boats are dangerous places."

She turned to the other people on the

table. "Hello," she said. "I'm Mary Ellen Connolly, and this is my brother, Frankie."

"Sholem aleichem," said a young girl about Mary Ellen's age, "Hello."

"Do you speak English?" asked Frankie.

"A little," said the girl. "My name is Hannah. We are Jews, from Russia."

"Why are you going to America?" Frankie asked.

"Why is anyone?" answered Hannah.

"For a better life. To find a place where no one calls you names or pulls your hair or throws rocks at you."

They sat talking after they had finished eating, and when Hannah told them about the night their house was burnt down and their baby brother died there was a long silence.

"So the Irish aren't the only ones who've suffered," said Mary Ellen at last, turning to Frankie. "And the English aren't the only ones to blame for the troubles of the world."

A young man of about sixteen was sitting opposite. He'd been listening all through the meal, and had stayed when everyone else left.

"My name is Sam and I'm English," he said quietly as Mary Ellen blushed. "I know some of the things that have happened in Ireland, and I'm not proud of them. But I think it's wrong to blame all my people for your troubles. My family are poor, just like everyone here. There was nothing for us at home, either, so we're going to California to find a better life."

Frankie went off, with a strict warning from Mary Ellen not to run on deck or go too near the railings. Then she and her two new friends followed him up, talking all evening and well into the night.

They shared their dreams and their fears until they were so cold they were forced to go back inside. Hannah led them down below and, after whispering to her mother, pulled out an old battered suitcase to show the family treasures they'd brought with them: two silver candlesticks, a beautifully embroidered tablecloth and a leather-bound Bible.

Later, as Mary Ellen lay in her bunk in the darkness, she thought about how much she was going to enjoy this voyage.

5

The Storm

It took Frankie and Mary Ellen a day or two to get used to the rolling of the sea. They were both seasick at first, but Sam showed them that the best place to be when you were feeling bad was up on deck, and from then on things weren't so bad.

The three teenagers spent as much time as possible up there. It was so much better than the hot stale air below. Their hair blew into their faces, and sometimes their words were cast to the wind so they had to talk in signs. As they told each other about all the bad things that had happened to them and their people, the sea breeze seemed to blow their stories into the past.

Mary Ellen enjoyed the company of her new friends so much that she forgot her promise to keep a close eye on her brother. Frankie took to wandering all over the boat, especially the forbidden First Class area. He was amazed how different it was. Everyone had their own cabin, and there was a smoking room, a saloon, a barber's shop, even a library. And the food!

He had to make sure no one saw him, of course, especially the crew. He knew his clothes made it obvious he wasn't First Class, and that he'd be in real trouble if he was caught. But Frankie was an expert at sneaking around without being seen - that was half the fun!

The fifth night the weather took a turn for the worse. It had been calm when they went to bed, but everyone slept badly.

Mary Ellen dreamed of little Liam and the twins calling her home, Frankie dreamed of his dog whining all night, Sam dreamed of being lost in the terrible heat of the California desert, and Hannah woke the whole cabin with her screams.

The ship was pitching and rolling, creaking and moaning. Mary Ellen took Hannah up on deck, to help her clear her head of the nightmares which were so horrible she refused even to talk about them.

They stood arm in arm in the stern of the ship, watching the storm rising, with Mary Ellen's shawl wrapped tight around their shoulders, until they realised a sailor was shouting at them angrily.

"Get back below, you two!" he yelled above the roaring sea. "There's bad weather on the way. No one's allowed on deck!"

They went below, and were surprised to find how much worse it felt. People were groaning, bundles were sliding across the floor and a bowl crashed off the table.

A child fell from her bunk and screamed for her mother. Mary Ellen saw an old woman with her rosary beads praying to be spared.

The storm was now at its height. The waves seemed to fling the giant liner from side to side like a toy and it creaked as though at any minute it might burst apart.

Yet, despite the danger, Mary Ellen wanted to be back on deck. She pleaded with Sam to go with her, and at last he agreed.

They clung tightly to the rails and to each other as the *Orlandia* climbed a dark cliff of water. They held their breath as the big ship hung on the top of the mighty wave, at the mercy of the sea. Then they screamed as she plunged down the other side, throwing great walls of spray across the ship and drenching them to the skin.

"Oh, I love the sea, Sam," Mary Ellen gasped as they dried out down below. "I love its power and its moods. I love the way it changes from one moment to the next and how you can never know it all or see it all."

"That's as maybe," said Sam, "but I'm a man of the soil myself. I can see the beauty of the sea, all right, but I'd rather watch its anger from dry land, thank you very much."

"My dad says, 'That's as maybe' just like that," said Mary Ellen, laughing. And it was at that moment she realised two things. That even though he was English, Sam was very like her father, and that maybe for the first time she was just a little bit in love.

6

Stop, Thief!

The next morning when Mary Ellen woke up, Frankie wasn't in his bunk. She asked Sam's younger brothers, but none of them had seen him. Sam and Hannah helped her search, but they couldn't see him anywhere. Mary Ellen described him to the first mate.

"Oh," he said, "that must be the wee monkey I found sneaking around earlier. Follow me." He led them to the Captain's cabin, where they discovered a worried Frankie. "So he's your brother, is he?" said the Captain. "I can't get a word out of him, the rascal. He was found in First Class with his pockets full of apples and oranges, and the first mate here thinks he stole them. If he did, then he won't be allowed into the United States, I'm afraid. They never take in thieves."

"My brother wouldn't steal," said Mary Ellen desperately, "Would you, Frankie?"

"No!" said Frankie.

"So where did you get the fruit, boy?" the Captain asked.

"I can't tell you."

"I think you'll have to, Frankie," said Mary Ellen. "Or we'll be going back to Ireland in disgrace."

"But if I tell I'll get my friend in trouble," said Frankie quietly.

Mary Ellen looked at the Captain.

"If you can prove no one's been

stealing, Frankie," the Captain said, "there'll be no trouble for anyone."

Frankie decided he'd have to trust the captain, and poured out the whole story.

"Fetch the Brookhams, please," the Captain told the first mate. Within a few minutes the sailor came back with three people Mary Ellen immediately recognised as the lady and gentleman she'd spoken to when they'd just arrived on board, and their nervous-looking son.

"What's all this about?" demanded the gentleman.

"I'm sorry to bother you, Lord Brookham, but this boy" – the Captain pointed at Frankie – "tells us that he's a friend of your son."

"Hah!" said Lady Brookham. "My Algernon wouldn't mix with people like that, would you, darling?"

Algie was silent.

"Francis Connolly here," continued the Captain, "was found in the First Class area, although he only has a ticket for steerage. His pockets were stuffed full of fruit. My first mate suspects he was stealing, but Francis tells us he was given it by your son."

"Algie?" said his mother. "Do you know anything about this?"

"I ought to tell you that stealing on board is a very serious offence," said the Captain.

"He didn't steal it!" said Algie, finding

his courage at last. "I gave it to him! He was hungry, and we get far more than we need."

Lord and Lady Brookham gasped, Frankie beamed with pleasure that his friend had stood up for him, and the Captain smiled.

"Thank you, first mate," said the Captain. "I shall be taking no further action. You can show everyone out."

7

The New World

"America! It's America!"

Frankie was the first to sight land. He flew down both flights of stairs to spread the news.

"It's America! I've seen it!"

Everyone rushed up behind him, and

he was right. There was
cheering and hugging and the tossing of
caps and babies into the air.

That morning the sailors had woken
everyone in steerage early, telling them to
pack their bags and prepare for landing.
The whole place had been a hive of
activity, with people washing and shaving
and putting on their best clothes. The
queues for the washrooms stretched all the
way down the corridor. But Frankie, who

wasn't too fussed about washing at the best of times, had hidden up on deck with Algie, and that's how they'd got to be the first to see the New World.

After a while Mary Ellen went back down to gather up her belongings. She found a gang of sailors scrubbing the floor and walls. All the staleness had gone, and the place smelt of disinfectant. Suddenly remembering Frankie's neck and the promise she'd made to her mother, she ran back up to find him.

"Just as I thought, Frankie Connolly," she said with a laugh, "a new suit on your back, yet enough mud on your neck to grow potatoes! Get into that washroom this minute and give yourself a good scrub or you're not getting off this ship, even if it means sailing all the way back to Ireland!"

As they got nearer, Mary Ellen could see ferry boats on the water and tall buildings in the background. In the foreground she could just make out a figure.

"It's the Statue of Liberty," said Sam at her side. She hadn't noticed him arrive, but she was glad he was there.

They watched as the statue grew in size until it was standing tall and proud above them, holding the torch of welcome. A great cheer went up and people began laughing, crying or praying, thanking God for a safe journey.

"It's a beautiful sight," said Sam, and Mary Ellen turned to him to agree, only to realise that he was looking, not at America, but at her in her best shawl! She blushed to the roots of her hair.

"I shall miss you, Mary Ellen," he said, reaching out and kissing her.

"And I shall miss you, Sam," she whispered when she'd recovered from the shock. "But what will people think?" she added, looking round, only to find that most other people were hugging and kissing too, in the joy of arrival.

At long last the boat docked.

"Where's Jim?" said Frankie, looking around. "He said he'd be here to meet us."

"Don't worry," said Mary Ellen, holding on to him tightly. "We've still got to take the ferry to Ellis Island, where America decides who they'll let in and who they'll send home."

"I couldn't bear to have come all this way and be sent back!" said Hannah at Mary Ellen's side.

"Why would they?" asked Frankie, worried.

"Only if you're very sick," said Sam, "or if you've no money and no means of getting any. Or if you're a criminal."

Everyone went quiet then, especially Frankie.

At Ellis Island they walked up the iron steps to the main building, where they were given a medical card and told to wait their turn. A giant United States flag hung above them.

One doctor lifted their eyelids, another inspected their faces and hands for skin disease, and so on. After each check they held out their card to be stamped.

Then there was another long wait. Someone got out a concertina and people danced to try and cover up their fear. Then they were called forward.

"Have you any relatives here?"

"Have you somewhere to live?"

"Have you a job to go to?"

"Have you ever been in jail?"

Questions, questions, questions.

At last the lucky ones were told, "Welcome to the United States of America. You're free to go."

Frankie had already said goodbye to Algie, who didn't have to go to Ellis Island as his family were only visiting America, rather than emigrating.

"Shalom aleichem, Hannah," said Mary Ellen, putting her arms around her friend. "Goodbye. I hope you're happy in Chicago."

Then she looked at Sam and saw that there were tears in his eyes too.

"I won't forget you, Mary Ellen," he said, kissing her, and this time in full view of everyone. "When I've enough money I'll

come to New York to see you. Would you like that?"

"Oh yes, Sam," said Mary Ellen. "I'd like it very much. I'll write back the very day, the very hour I get your letters!" she told both her friends, for she was the only one who had an address until the others reached their destinations.

But would they keep their promises, she thought? Would the excitement of their new life make them forget the friends they'd made on the way? Would Sam really remember her when there was the whole of America between them?

With minds full to bursting, of Ireland,

of the voyage and of the future, Mary Ellen and Frankie took the ferry to Manhattan, where their brother Jim and his new wife greeted them with open arms.

Emigration to America

Emigration

Over two million people left Ireland in the decade of the Potato Famine, 1846-55. From then on emigration became part of the expected pattern of life in Ireland, and it continued at a high rate until very recently. In a hundred years more people left Ireland than now live there. They went mainly to the United States, Britain, Canada and Australia. Almost all Irish emigrants were young and unmarried and at least half were women. People went from all over the country, but mainly from the poorer, farming areas especially in the West. They left because there was a much better chance of employment abroad.

The Irish were not the only people to emigrate to America in large numbers. Between 1830 and 1930, 35 million Europeans sailed west for a new life.

American Wakes

The night before emigrants left, a party would be held in their house to see them off. In different areas of Ireland this was known as a live wake, a parting spree, a farewell supper, a convoy, a feast of departure and, in Donegal, an American bottle night. A wake in Ireland was the ancient custom of watching with the dead overnight until burial the next day, usually with the help of friends, neighbours, drink and music. It was supposed to ward off evil spirits. The party to see emigrants off was known as a wake because those leaving were quite likely never to return.

An American wake would start at nightfall and last until the early hours. There would be music and dancing, songs and stories. Despite their sadness it was also seen by many as a celebration: the start of a new and better life.

Steamships

Steamships began to cross the Atlantic from the late 1860s, but people found it hard to forget the horrors of the sailing ships of the Famine years. These had come to be known as 'coffin ships' due to the terrible conditions on board and the great numbers who died of fever or shipwreck.

Steamships sailing from Liverpool, and calling in at Queenstown on the south coast of Ireland, would have carried English and Irish emigrants, plus some from Russia, Northern and Eastern Europe.

By the time this story is set, the voyage would have taken eight to twelve days and cost about £5 for those travelling steerage. First and Second Class passengers paid extra and had a much more comfortable journey.

The Jews

From the 1890s onwards there was massive emigration to America from Central and Eastern

Europe. Very many of the emigrants were Jews, who had faced terrible discrimination, hostility and violence in their home countries.

"Shalom aleichem" means both hello and goodbye in Yiddish, the language they used.

Ellis Island

To prevent emigrants bringing in fever, and to stop those who had no money from entering the country, the American authorities set up a landing depot on Ellis Island in 1892. Although there was a hospital, you could change your money into dollars, buy rail tickets and get advice on finding lodgings and work, Ellis Island had a reputation for herding people around like cattle, and was feared by those arriving.

Sparks: Historical Adventures

ANCIENT GREECE

The Great Horse of Troy – The Trojan War
0 7496 3369 7 (hbk) 0 7496 3538 X (pbk)
The Winner's Wreath – Ancient Greek Olympics
0 7496 3368 9 (hbk) 0 7496 3555 X (pbk)

INVADERS AND SETTLERS

Boudicca Strikes Back – The Romans in Britain
0 7496 3366 2 (hbk) 0 7496 3546 0 (pbk)
Viking Raiders – A Norse Attack
0 7496 3089 2 (hbk) 0 7496 3457 X (pbk)
Erik's New Home – A Viking Town
0 7496 3367 0 (hbk) 0 7496 3552 5 (pbk)

TALES OF THE ROWDY ROMANS

The Great Necklace Hunt
0 7496 2221 0 (hbk) 0 7496 2628 3 (pbk)
The Lost Legionary
0 7496 2222 9 (hbk) 0 7496 2629 1 (pbk)
The Guard Dog Geese
0 7496 2331 4 (hbk) 0 7496 2630 5 (pbk)
A Runaway Donkey
0 7496 2332 2 (hbk) 0 7496 2631 3 (pbk)

TUDORS AND STUARTS

Captain Drake's Orders – The Armada
0 7496 2556 2 (hbk) 0 7496 3121 X (pbk)
London's Burning – The Great Fire of London
0 7496 2557 0 (hbk) 0 7496 3122 8 (pbk)
Mystery at the Globe – Shakespeare's Theatre
0 7496 3096 5 (hbk) 0 7496 3449 9 (pbk)
Plague! – A Tudor Epidemic
0 7496 3365 4 (hbk) 0 7496 3556 8 (pbk)
Stranger in the Glen – Rob Roy
0 7496 2586 4 (hbk) 0 7496 3123 6 (pbk)
A Dream of Danger – The Massacre of Glencoe
0 7496 2587 2 (hbk) 0 7496 3124 4 (pbk)
A Queen's Promise – Mary Queen of Scots
0 7496 2589 9 (hbk) 0 7496 3125 2 (pbk)
Over the Sea to Skye – Bonnie Prince Charlie
0 7496 2588 0 (hbk) 0 7496 3126 0 (pbk)

TALES OF A TUDOR TEARAWAY

A Pig Called Henry
0 7496 2204 4 (hbk) 0 7496 2625 9 (pbk)
A Horse Called Deathblow
0 7496 2205 9 (hbk) 0 7496 2624 0 (pbk)
Dancing for Captain Drake
0 7496 2234 2 (hbk) 0 7496 2626 7 (pbk)
Birthdays are a Serious Business
0 7496 2235 0 (hbk) 0 7496 2627 5 (pbk)

VICTORIAN ERA

The Runaway Slave – The British Slave Trade
0 7496 3093 0 (hbk) 0 7496 3456 1 (pbk)
The Sewer Sleuth – Victorian Cholera
0 7496 2590 2 (hbk) 0 7496 3128 7 (pbk)
Convict! – Criminals Sent to Australia
0 7496 2591 0 (hbk) 0 7496 3129 5 (pbk)
An Indian Adventure – Victorian India
0 7496 3090 6 (hbk) 0 7496 3451 0 (pbk)
Farewell to Ireland – Emigration to America
0 7496 3094 9 (hbk) 0 7496 3448 0 (pbk)
The Great Hunger – Famine in Ireland
0 7496 3095 7 (hbk) 0 7496 3447 2 (pbk)
Fire Down the Pit – A Welsh Mining Disaster
0 7496 3091 4 (hbk) 0 7496 3450 2 (pbk)
Tunnel Rescue – The Great Western Railway
0 7496 3353 0 (hbk) 0 7496 3537 1 (pbk)
Kidnap on the Canal – Victorian Waterways
0 7496 3352 2 (hbk) 0 7496 3540 1 (pbk)
Dr. Barnardo's Boys – Victorian Charity
0 7496 3358 1 (hbk) 0 7496 3541 X (pbk)
The Iron Ship – Brunel's Great Britain
0 7496 3355 7 (hbk) 0 7496 3543 6 (pbk)
Bodies for Sale – Victorian Tomb-Robbers
0 7496 3364 6 (hbk) 0 7496 3539 8 (pbk)
Penny Post Boy – The Victorian Postal Service
0 7496 3362 X (hbk) 0 7496 3544 4 (pbk)
The Canal Diggers – The Manchester Ship Canal
0 7496 3356 5 (hbk) 0 7496 3545 2 (pbk)
The Tay Bridge Tragedy – A Victorian Disaster
0 7496 3354 9 (hbk) 0 7496 3547 9 (pbk)
Stop, Thief! – The Victorian Police
0 7496 3359 X (hbk) 0 7496 3548 7 (pbk)
Miss Buss and Miss Beale – Victorian Schools
0 7496 3360 3 (hbk) 0 7496 3549 5 (pbk)
Chimney Charlie – Victorian Chimney Sweeps
0 7496 3351 4 (hbk) 0 7496 3551 7 (pbk)
Down the Drain – Victorian Sewers
0 7496 3357 3 (hbk) 0 7496 3550 9 (pbk)
The Ideal Home – A Victorian New Town
0 7496 3361 1 (hbk) 0 7496 3553 3 (pbk)
Stage Struck – Victorian Music Hall
0 7496 3363 8 (hbk) 0 7496 3554 1 (pbk)

TRAVELS OF A YOUNG VICTORIAN

The Golden Key
0 7496 2360 8 (hbk) 0 7496 2632 1 (pbk)
Poppy's Big Push
0 7496 2361 6 (hbk) 0 7496 2633 X (pbk)
Poppy's Secret
0 7496 2374 8 (hbk) 0 7496 2634 8 (pbk)
The Lost Treasure
0 7496 2375 6 (hbk) 0 7496 2635 6 (pbk)

20th-CENTURY HISTORY

Fight for the Vote – The Suffragettes
0 7496 3092 2 (hbk) 0 7496 3452 9 (pbk)
The Road to London – The Jarrow March
0 7496 2609 7 (hbk) 0 7496 3132 5 (pbk)
The Sandbag Secret – The Blitz
0 7496 2608 9 (hbk) 0 7496 3133 3 (pbk)
Sid's War – Evacuation
0 7496 3209 7 (hbk) 0 7496 3445 6 (pbk)
D-Day! – Wartime Adventure
0 7496 3208 9 (hbk) 0 7496 3446 4 (pbk)
The Prisoner – A Prisoner of War
0 7496 3212 7 (hbk) 0 7496 3455 3 (pbk)
Escape from Germany – Wartime Refugees
0 7496 3211 9 (hbk) 0 7496 3454 5 (pbk)
Flying Bombs – Wartime Bomb Disposal
0 7496 3210 0 (hbk) 0 7496 3453 7 (pbk)
12,000 Miles From Home – Sent to Australia
0 7496 3370 0 (hbk) 0 7496 3542 8 (pbk)